Dear Parents and Educators,

Welcome to Penguin Young Readers! As parents and educators, you know that each child develops at his or her own pace—in terms of speech, critical thinking, and, of course, reading. Penguin Young Readers recognizes this fact. As a result, each Penguin Young Readers book is assigned a traditional easy-to-read level (1–4) as well as a Guided Reading Level (A–P). Both of these systems will help you choose the right book for your child. Please refer to the back of each book for specific leveling information. Penguin Young Readers features esteemed authors and illustrators, stories about favorite characters, fascinating nonfiction, and more!

Bad Hair Day

LEVEL 2

GUIDED READING LEVEL **F**

This book is perfect for a **Progressing Reader** who:
- can figure out unknown words by using picture and context clues;
- can recognize beginning, middle, and ending sounds;
- can make and confirm predictions about what will happen in the text; and
- can distinguish between fiction and nonfiction.

Here are some **activities** you can do during and after reading this book:
- Word Repetition: The author repeats the words *snip* and *clip* throughout the story. Reread the story and count how many times each word is used.
- The illustrator has drawn lots of pictures of funny hairstyles such as a beehive, hair with streaks, and too-tight perms. On a separate piece of paper, draw pictures of the funniest hairdos you can imagine.
- Rhyming Words: Find the rhyming words in the story. On a separate sheet of paper, write each word next to the word it rhymes with. Use the chart below as an example.

Word	Rhymes with
see	me
snip	clip

Remember, sharing the love of reading with a child is the best gift you can give!

—Bonnie Bader, EdM, and Katie Carella, EdM
Penguin Young Readers program

*Penguin Young Readers are leveled by independent reviewers applying the standards developed by Irene Fountas and Gay Su Pinnell in *Matching Books to Readers: Using Leveled Books in Guided Reading*, Heinemann, 1999.

For my mom—SH

To my son Fred,
who endured his mom's buzz cuts!—JA

Penguin Young Readers
Published by the Penguin Group
Penguin Group (USA) Inc., 375 Hudson Street, New York, New York 10014, USA
Penguin Group (Canada), 90 Eglinton Avenue East, Suite 700, Toronto, Ontario M4P 2Y3, Canada
(a division of Pearson Penguin Canada Inc.)
Penguin Books Ltd., 80 Strand, London WC2R 0RL, England
Penguin Group Ireland, 25 St. Stephen's Green, Dublin 2, Ireland (a division of Penguin Books Ltd.)
Penguin Group (Australia), 250 Camberwell Road, Camberwell, Victoria 3124, Australia
(a division of Pearson Australia Group Pty. Ltd.)
Penguin Books India Pvt. Ltd., 11 Community Centre, Panchsheel Park, New Delhi—110 017, India
Penguin Group (NZ), 67 Apollo Drive, Rosedale, Auckland 0632, New Zealand
(a division of Pearson New Zealand Ltd.)
Penguin Books (South Africa) (Pty.) Ltd., 24 Sturdee Avenue,
Rosebank, Johannesburg 2196, South Africa

Penguin Books Ltd., Registered Offices: 80 Strand, London WC2R 0RL, England

Text copyright © 1999 by Susan Hood. Illustrations copyright © 1999 by Joy Allen. All rights reserved. First published in 1999 by Grosset & Dunlap, an imprint of Penguin Group (USA) Inc. Published in 2011 by Penguin Young Readers, an imprint of Penguin Group (USA) Inc., 345 Hudson Street, New York, New York 10014. Manufactured in China.

Library of Congress Control Number: 99020901

ISBN 978-0-448-41996-1   10 9 8 7 6 5 4 3 2 1

Bad Hair Day

Happy reading!

Susan Hood

by Susan Hood
illustrated by Joy Allen

Penguin Young Readers
An Imprint of Penguin Group (USA) Inc.

My hair is long.

I cannot see.

My mother says,

"Please, come with me."

My mother says,

"Just a snip!"

Her scissors go

clip, clip, clip.

Oops! My bangs
are out of line.

8

My mom says, "Wait!

Just give me time."

Snip, snip, snip.

Clip, clip, clip.

Now my bangs take a dip!

One side is up.

One side is down.

I grab my hat.

We walk to town.

"We will fix it," says my mom.

"We will go to Mister Tom.

Please do not fret and do not fuss.

Bad hair days come to all of us!"

I look and see

that it is true.

Not all hair does

what it should do.

Some hair sticks up

in the air,

giving people

quite a scare!

Crazy curls

from too-tight perms

bob along like

wiggly worms!

There is hair

that's pink and blue,

a beehive, and

a bird's nest, too!

Her hair has streaks.

His hair is flat.

I'm glad my hair

is not like that!

One man's hair

just blows away!

For him, today's

a **no** hair day!

Mister Tom says,

"Just a snip."

His scissors go

clip, clip, clip!

I wear my hat
to school next day.
What will kids think?
What will they say?

My teacher says,

"Hats off, please."

Will kids laugh?

Will they tease?

Surprise! Surprise!

A good hair day!

The kids ALL want

their hair this way!